Love To Say Goodbye

Charles Rhodes Jamison

Dedicated to the love of my life, once tacit teacher now divine leader-Bailey.

*T*ires come to a screeching halt outside a hospital. A man dressed in corduroy leaps out of a worn out vehicle. Running around the trunk he quickly opens the door for a pregnant passenger. Three attendants exit the front doors assisting the hasty driver. Entering the hospital, the helping trio rolls in pregnant woman. She smiles while wrapping both hands around her belly. All four hustle inside, except soon to be father. The grown man with short brown hair, clad in brown, raises his arms to the sky in thanks for their safe arrival. He snaps out of his momentary spell then strides swiftly through the entrance. A female nurse in the lobby matches father's excitement and urgency. She ushers him down the hallway, father enters to hold mother's hand firmly all the way to the end.

Baby cries, a child is born...hallelujah.
The friendly nurse escorts messy infant to be cleaned. The father's arms kindly reach out to the mother. The Doctor informs the new parents of their healthy newborn son while removing soiled gloves. The matronly doctor reaches for a birth certificate. She stands and addresses the parents, "What's the name of your dear child?"

The Mother and Father look at each other fondly responding together, "Thomas."

Years later, young Thomas (Tommy) stands on a street corner, near his home. As the school bus approaches, Tommy hears faint laughter from the school children before bus arrives. The bus driver stops to pick up Tommy. Tommy's mother runs from the porch calling out to Tommy,

"You forgot your lunch, Tommy."

His mother plays a quick cat and mouse game with Tommy. Tommy lunges forward and their hands come together. Tommy's mother gives him a quick kiss. Off to school goes the boy attired with blue jeans and white T-shirt.

Tommy fetches academic books from his locker. A student in the hall gives Tommy a little shove. Tommy doesn't care since the kid's obnoxious. He snickers always and whispers to others when Tommy is around. Not the coolest guy in school, Tommy never says the right words in front of girls. Most of the time he clams up and downright freezes. Tommy's classmates giggle at him, chanting and relentlessly stating their cruel motto, "You will never have friends, Tommy."

The bell rings and students are dismissed, school day ends; because time flies.

Tommy sits at the dinner table with his mother and father. The family eats supper and his parents chat about their day. His parents ask him if he has made any new friends. His mother and father explain the importance of having friends. Tommy excuses himself to make his own desert. His parents continue playing their broken record,

"Only if you promise to make friends."

Tommy responds,

"I will do my best."

The choice desert for Tommy: white bread, peanut butter and sliced banana, never toasted.

Tommy merrily goes upstairs to his bedroom. He sits on tile floor in front of small television. He ponders while gazing at the television with his sandwich. As he reaches to turn on the television, Tommy hesitates. He imagines a hand next to his, then a green forearm to an elbow next to his arm. Both hands turn television knob simultaneously.

Tommy's favorite comedy appears and Tommy gives his newly created friend a high five making a magical chime. Sparkling glitter materializes and a figure takes shape. The two mimic the scenes on the television and chuckle together. The imaginary friend asks,

"What is your name?"

Tommy replies,

"They call me Tommy."

His novel pal again,

"How about we call you Tom?"

Tommy answers,

"Yeah, I like Tom."

His friend says,

"Congratulations, you have made yourself a friend."

Tommy splits his sandwich making halves. A full moon shines in the bedroom mirror as the two watch TV.

For years Thomas keeps to himself, relying more on his imagination than others.

Grade school ends, college begins. Tommy's parents bring him to the local train station. The conductor has his hand on the horn. He waits and tries to be patient as he witnesses the family's goodbyes.

"Now Tommy you are going to make real friends, right?"

Tommy's mother talks some more,

"You are going to say goodbye to the imaginary friend you created right son?"

His mother edifies rapidly. She reminds him to clean his teeth, write to her and tops off with,

"Let me know if you need more towels or food."

Tommy's father speaks over his mother to state,

"Remember to be a good boy."

The conductor toots his horn and begins impishly blowing his whistle. The conductor and father glare at each other. Tommy twiddles to make his way on the train. Tommy's father blurts out lastly, "Tommy, remember don't ever become angry."

Tommy waves farewell at train's doorstep. Mother and father call out, "Goodbye son."

His parents watch the train depart, still gazing at lingering smoke trail from the train. They both stare in the distance until another train startles them. They laugh together.

A new place around unfamiliar people, Thomas refers himself as Tom to everybody he meets. Soon Tom enters a house party filled with foggy haze and students coughing. As Tom walks down a hallway, a passing party goer rudely murmurs,

"Go home Tom."

Tom pauses and looks down the end of the hall. He sees his imaginary friend in the mirror. His imaginary friend declares,

"We can't have that."

Tom spins around and positions his back against the mirror. Tom utters to himself,

"So what do you suggest we do?" The fictitous reflection beside him incites by whispering, "Retaliate." Tom announces down the hall,

"Hey buddy, I hear they call you 'The Eunuch from Munich'."

Tom snarls at the bully provoking a slow walk towards each other to face off. The bully (close enough to smell breath) jaws at Tom,

"Well Tom, at least I don't walk around talking to an imaginary friend."

Tom retorts,

"At least I can make friends by having balls. I hear the only thing you can make wet is your bed."

Tom continues to the bully,

"You don't have a sack nor a pack, Eunuch from Munich." The bully treads away with his head slightly down feeling somewhat defeated. A few jocks come out of a room, right outside the confrontation. Tom questions his unreal friend,

"Now what do I do?"

His Imaginary friend raises both of Tom's arms. The partiers pat Tom on his shoulders in a congratulatory manner.

On registration day, Tom stands under a shaded tree with his fictional friend on campus. The students are loitering as they register for classes. Tom explains to sidekick,

"I have a lot on my schedule. I need to lighten my load. We will never have time to watch TV and eat our sandwiches."

Tom's imaginary shadow agrees with Tom then suggests,

"Sign up for Art, that is an easy A."

Tom advances to a kiosk which has a sign (above the entrance) depicting two hands holding the earth. A female student with curly red hair, tied wildly by ribbons engages Tom,

"Hey do you like gardening too?"

Tom replies,

"Depends…would you say this is an easy course?"

She responds,

"Easy, relaxing and fun."

Tom gazes to his left first,

"Well sign me up."

Later that day, Tom bursts into a classroom with a huge smile on his face. He boisterously apologizes to the teacher and the class. On his way to sit, at the only seat available he utters indirectly,

"I tried several classes, first Geometry, then Geology and I finally got it at Gardening."

The teacher places a book on his desk. Tom smirks and crumples a piece of paper. He catches the eye of a girl staring at him intensely. Tom cocks back his arm to throw a crumpled piece of paper. He observes the girl and she slowly turns her head from side to side, tacitly telling Tom to stop. Tom pauses with a quizzical expression. He begins to mimic her head shaking actions. While doing so, his imaginary friend sticks his head in front of Tom blocking the girl. His imaginary friend glances back and forth from Tom to the girl. Grinning at the girl, Tom lowers his arm to restore his paper. The girl gestures with pointed finger signaling approval for that course of action.

Tom fires into his dorm room after class. He grabs a snack. Noticing his roommate is fidgety, uptight and pacing about the small quarters, he opens a window. His roommate broods over whether he chose the right classes and complains about the up-coming semester. Tom converses softly,

"Let's get out, college isn't all about classes and books. We should hit a dance party and make all the students think the world shook."

Tom's roommate fancies the spontaneous idea questioning,

"Well do you know of anything?"

Tom thinks….then speaks,

"Well I know that door opens and if we open it, limbs might too."   Tom and his roommate exit their room, briskly moving down steps with a skip and a hop. Out the main door, the duo make their way to a corner. Tom's imaginary friend tugs at Tom. Tom hits him back. The roommate wears all black except a red tie loosely hanging from his neck. He looks at Tom who has on a brown jacket atop jeans,

"What is with that? Is that Turrets or a nervous tick?"

Tom rebuts,

"Dancing makes me nervous. I don't think I have the right moves."

Earlier, Tom took notice of flyers on a tree denoting an all welcome party at the communal hall.

They arrive at their destination. Upon entering, Tom's chimerical acquaintance reaches for the television in the small sitting area. Tom begins to concede moving forward. The song, "Never Gonna Leave This Bed"   by   Maroon Five plays which needless to convey is a great song. He instantly locks eyes with a young woman dressed in red. Once locked, the familiar girl with red hair makes an intense gesture of shooting a pistol. Tom imitates her.

The girl begins to slowly circle around the perimeter of the room. Stuck in a trance, Tom shadows and goes in opposite direction. He keeps his eyes fixed on the intriguing female. They sway back and forth, moving to the music. As they make their approach, each reach for the other's hand. Tom touches her hand. His imaginary friend grabs Tom's other hand pulling he from she.   Tom shakes off unrealistic grasp forceful enough to create a slap sound hitting the girls other palm. At the same time they both say, "Hello."

A lightning bolt instantly knocks out the lights and music. Two DJ's on stage scramble to determine how to keep the party going. One of the DJ's shakes   and   kicks his equipment. The other DJ becomes mad. He naturally settles down when a cute admirer fondles his instrument.

A strong gust of wind blows open the ballroom doors. Guests babble amongst themselves while torrential downpour exists. Tom smiles then addresses dance partner,

"Where is your domain dame?"

She responds,

"Just two streets over on Madison."

Tom spots his unsubstantial friend shivering, soaked and holding his head down across the street. Tom removes his jacket. He drapes the jacket over his dance partner's head and takes her hand. Tom smirks,

"Let's get you home."

They hustle through the streets and around a bend. A car horn beeps. A black muscle car drives up to roll down its window. Rod (Tom's roommate) shouts from the driver seat,

"Hop in."

The girl with Tom takes her foot and flirtatiously splashes Tom with the help of a puddle. Tom calls back to Rod,

"Unless you have a change of clothes or dry towels, we will make it on foot." The girl swings Tom's jacket as they galavant down a campus street. The pair is soaked by rain and joy when they reach Madison avenue. Near the end of their walk, the car stops ahead. A female hops out of Rod's car. She runs up the steps. The one with Tom yells,

"Samantha, I will see you upstairs."

Tom's roommate edges his car up. Rod adjusts his mirrors to sneak a peek. Tom swallows, bites his bottom lip before communicating,

"I was intrigued by your glance and tonight, delighted by our dance. I am known as Tom." The female same as always, curly red hair, adorned flossily with red ribbons,

"I am Laura, pleasure to meet you, Tom. May I call you Thomas?" Tom nods enthusiastically,

"I like Thomas."

Laura heads inside.

Tom skips down steps. Rod pops the ride in reverse, he warns,

"You are bound to end up dead or catch a cold out here."

Tom stares to his left and right before replying,

"I don't think so, I have a warm heart tonight."

Rod chuckles,

"Get in Romeo."

They drive off leaving a trail of smoke from the car's tailpipe along with Thomas' jilted, drenched and cold imaginary friend standing below a waning crescent moon. Rod and Tom enter their dorm. They grab a few snacks and dry themselves. Rod takes a bite,

"It was a good night, but it was cut kinda short."

Tom, eating his granola bar,

"Yeah, it is early."

A sudden knock on the door and Rod answers. The resident manager, holding a piece of paper,

"I have a letter for Thomas."

Tom jumps up,

"That is for me."

Rod questions,

"But you are not Thomas."

Tom again,

"I am Tom, Thomas too."

The resident manager clarifies,

"I have to get this to Thomas."

Tom insistently,

"Give me my letter."

After a quick snag, he peruses the paper,

"The night just got younger."

Tom and Rod spurred on by a second wind, leave their room wearing fresh clothes. Car headlights come to a stop. Two young women dressed in clean attire, not ready to retire, enter vehicle. Samantha, wearing a red sweater (twirling her long dark hair) directs her attention to Tom,

"You must be Thomas."

Tom fires back,

"You must be Samantha."

Laura clad in a purple top and white shorts, speaks to Rod in driver's seat,
"You must be Rod, Thomas' roommate."
Rod joins the impromptu conversation,
"And you must be Laura."
Laura chimes in,
"I should be but I am not."
They all laugh and car pulls away. Tom's unreal pal sulks with his arms crossed, appearing somber in the middle of the dark street.

They arrive at a restaurant near campus. A bubbly hostess seats the four at an outside patio. The waitress takes their order and gathers the menus. Rod speaks to Thomas, "So Thomas have you told Laura about your imaginary friend?"

The table goes silent. Rod breaks the silence and continues,
"Well, I guess not."
In order to appease the group, Samantha horns in asking,
"What imaginary friend?"
The waitress brings a basket and places bread on the table. Thomas reaches for the bread basket as his imaginary wraith materializes and reaches with Thomas. Thomas grabs a slice of bread. Thomas cocks the bread back playfully grinning at Rod. Thomas pauses and extends his forearm to Laura,
"Would you like some bread, Laura?"
Laura accepts, mainly to begin feeding the fish in the nearby pond below. She speaks to table,
" I don't know about you guys, but I am out of water. Everyone's glasses are almost empty and we are going to need more bread."
Rod throws back the beers. He also drinks a couple of shots. A tune begins playing. Samantha starts bobbing up and down in her seat and says repeatedly,
"I want to dance."
Rod and Samantha stand up in sync. They strut to the dance floor. Samantha turns at Laura before leaving the table,
" Want to dance with your new
friend?" Laura waves off Samantha,
"No I'm good, I'm taped out."
Rod and Samantha start grooving.

Thomas expresses to Laura,

"Samantha seems a little different."

Laura acknowledges,

"Samantha has one problem; she knows what she wants and she wants it now."

Thomas replies,

"So how about you, do you know what you want?"

Laura answers,

"I might, but I don't want it now. I want it forever."

The statement sits with them while Thomas heeds an angler on the other side of the pond's shore. The angler is on the shore adjusting his reel and straightening the line. He appears agitated as he untangles his mess. Thomas gazes at the water then verbalizes to Laura,

"You certainly attract fish."

Stopping in the middle of a killer dance move, Samantha yells from the dance floor,

"Rod, I want you off that stage right now!"

The waitress brings the checks and their dinners in doggy bags with a message,

"Here is your food and you need to settle up because we are going to close soon. Your friends appear ready for home and frankly so do I."

The waitress begins moving away. She leans over the railing,

"Hm, I didn't think there were any fish in that water."

Thomas, Laura, Samantha and Rod exit the restaurant happily. They make their way to Rod's car parked near the fisherman's truck. Rod hands over his keys to Thomas and tells him how to drive his car. Rod explains,

"You have to start it gently and turn the key slowly. I have not changed the oil or had a tune up recently. The steering is a little quirky."

Samantha, rolling her eyes,

"Just stop and give Thomas the keys."

The previous angler storms to his parked truck. He hastily packs up his gear. His wife has a cooler. She shows him the wine bottle and two glasses.

The angler throws his gear in the back of his truck. His wife sweetly implores,

"I thought we were going to have our wine and dish."

Thomas stares at the angry angler making a ruckus. The fisherman announces,

"Not when I am angry."

The four of them sit in Rod's car. Thomas struggles with the clutch. Laura studies Thomas' grip. Laura places her hand on Thomas'. An induced pause brought on by Laura's cool and steady touch, together they shift the car into gear. Thomas releases his foot off the brake and they slowly drive away.

Thomas and Rod drop the gals off at their dorm. The guys return to their domicile. Thomas helps Rod as he steps out of the car and fully assists Rod to their room. Rod plops down on his bed while Thomas grabs the chain to switch the light off.

Oh yea, morning dawns. Thomas leaps off the top bunk and pulls the light chain. Once light shines, Thomas spies his pretend buddy sitting at the television. Thomas blows past the made-up figure to grab a book. He leaves and saunters to class.

Tardy again, Thomas enters the classroom. Thomas earnestly apologizes to the teacher and classroom while searching for a vacant spot. The teacher takes over his voice,

"I know you are happening and we know you have an interesting life, you may also take a seat."

The teacher nattily clad, adjusting her giant spectacles goes on,

"I am splitting the classroom into parties… sorry I mean groups. We have an outdoor project."

The teacher places Thomas and Laura in the same group. Thomas tilts his head grinning at Laura,

"Well, what are the odds?"

The teacher places a plant on each groups' table while instructing her class,

"Your assignment is to keep your plant alive the entire semester."

The students carry on discussions about maintaining a plant. Laura makes a suggestion to her group,

"First, let's get to know the plant and then we will know what the plant likes."

Another girl within the group speaks up,

"Okay one of us must take the plant to their place tonight. I can't because my roommate went gothic and well...don't get me started, but there is no light whatsoever. My place resembles a cave." The other guy among the group stares at the plant when the same girl states,

"This guy can't take it to his place either. I know that gleam in his eye. He will smoke the plant."

The dude plucks a leaf from the plant. He tucks the leaf in his pocket articulating,

"I will do my part tonight."

Laura slides the plant over to Thomas asking,

"What do you say, Thomas, can you take the plant to your place tonight?"

Thomas wraps both hands around the plant, scoots the pot closer, "Yes, I will do my best. Some water, right amount of light, should be alright."

Thomas exits class. After a brisk walk, he enters his dorm room. He carefully sets the plant on a shelf near the window. Rod stumbles out of bed and walks unsteadily to a chair. He belches and flounders down on an old wooden chair. He mutters as he extends his arm and points from the chair,

"Where did that thing come from?"

Thomas instructs,

"This plant must not be disturbed."

Rod probes,

"Well, where did it come from?"

Thomas, now annoyed,

"The plant came from my class."

Rod wonders aloud,

"So, how about the two girls last night?"

Thomas replies,

"Yeah, are you going to see Samantha again?"

Rod hangs his head over the chair,

"I don't know."

A frisbee hits the window. Thomas rises to raise the window and spots the frisbee dangling from the gutter. He reaches for the frisbee and notices a student standing on the lawn. He waves up to Thomas who leans out the window. Holding on tight so he does not fall, Thomas snags the frisbee. Rod, slouched in the chair, lifts his arm for the whiskey bottle and pours some in a cup. He stirs the whiskey with his dirty finger. Thomas launches the frisbee from his window to the student below. Thomas stands at the door to leave. He questions Rod,

"Do you want to participate and have a good time? This seems like fun."

Rod rolls his lips similar to a horse declaring,

"Nope, I am going to take the edge off from last night."

Thomas, while closing the door, witnesses his delusional figment pointing at the television.

Thomas runs outside on the grass immediately becoming involved in the game. He catches and tosses the frisbee to one of the team mates. The opposing team acquires the frisbee, snatches and throws a long shot which lands out of bounds. Thomas with youthful energy springs at the chance to retrieve,

"I'll get it."

As Thomas tracks down flying saucer, a baseball rolls next to the frisbee. Laura appears jogging for the ball by his feet,

"Hey Laura."

"Hey Thomas, how is the plant?"

They both gather equipment.

Laura, walking away, shouts to Thomas,

"I do not like softball. I would rather be seen clean."

Thomas looks back at Laura,

"I think you appear great dirty. I will see you in class."

Thomas pitches the frisbee to the field. He puts too much loft on the throw so the frisbee gets lodged in the crevice of the campus clock tower. The bell on the clock tower chimes tolling a new period. Eager to return playing, Thomas runs through the playing field. Busting through the front doors of the campus clocktower, Thomas sprints up the stairs. After all he was just getting the hang of the game. Once at the narrow top, Thomas clings to the brick wall. He views the frisbee on the ledge. Still holding tight, Thomas does his best to knock the frisbee loose using his foot. His strategy fails, hence he lets go of the brick wall's foundation to grab a short iron gate. Unsteady and wobbly now, Thomas keeps his eyes on the frisbee. He seizes the round piece of plastic with one hand which causes him to slip and fall over the ledge. Thomas clings for dear life one hundred feet from the ground. One arm wrapped around the iron gate, the other hand barely keeps its grasp. Thomas (scared and sweating) becomes nervous but his imaginary friend breaks through Thomas' fear, insisting he let go and take his hand. Deep down Thomas knows he will fall without a hand on the rock. Therefore he shakes his head and adjusts his grip to secure either foot in a cranny. This allows him a moment to catch his breath. The imaginary friend waits with an offered palm calmly atop. Thomas won't budge. A crowd below begins to gather. Shouting takes place. Someone yells out an inappropriate joke about Thomas going ahead and jumping. Although facing death on top of insensitive pricks, Thomas remains motionless to prevent falling. Darting from the woods flies a young woman sporting a baseball uniform. She throws her hat to the ground while cursing the mean crowd. Laura jets upstairs. She comes to the rescue just in time, scattering the imaginary fog that makes up Thomas' fake friend. After lifting Thomas to safety, the two sit exhausted. Laura clears the air joking,

"I thought you could use a hand."

Thomas and Rod attend their graduation ceremony. Rod pours whiskey into his nasty cup from his flask. Thomas warns softly,

"Hey, can you take it easy? We are almost out of here."

Thomas goes on the stage and accepts his diploma from the dean. He and the dean shake hands. College comes to a close. From a decent education, he moves on to start a life.

Thomas sits at a young bankers desk. The banker gladly felicitates Thomas,

"Congratulations on your new home, Mr Dalton."

The banker thanks Thomas for his business. Then he accompanies Thomas through the lobby to the front entrance. The two are standing at the bank's front entry, when an impressive woman enters the bank. Thomas opens the door, tips his hat,

"Madam."

She thanks Thomas for opening the door. Thomas steps outside. A man walking past the bank sees Thomas commenting,

"Good Day, Mr Dalton."

A church bell chimes from across the street, interrupting Thomas' response,

"Good Day."

Thomas parks his truck at the driveway. He begins to unload a few items and carry them into his new home. He sets up his stereo and places the needle on the record to play, Billy Joel, "For The Longest Time." Thomas steps to the front door to finish unloading his truck. Laura stands on the front stoop. She holds a plant with the base at her hip, foliage blocking her face, "Thomas, you still have the plant."

Thomas laughs because he can't behold her remarking,

"Our love still grows."

Laura, adjusting the plant in her arms,

"Please allow me to find the proper spot."

Laura sets the plant on the kitchen table,

"I am so sorry to hear about Rod."

Thomas becomes solemn,

"Me too, I always knew it was going to be his car or the drink that kills him, but I never thought a combination of the two... wish I could have said goodbye."

Laura swings a bag from her shoulder, flopping it on the table. She takes out two wine glasses, uncorks the bottle and decants to toast,

"Is that right? Well, to us for being able to say goodbye."

They cling their glasses and move outdoors to enjoy the sunset. Laura and Thomas then enjoy a warm cup of tea by the fireplace before bedtime.

Thomas awakes at sunrise and shimmies to the end of the bed. He stretches his arm to touch the dial on the television. Laura reaches over and gives Thomas a morning hug and rolls back into bed. Thomas arises out of bed. He putters into the kitchen to make a peanut butter and banana sandwich. Once finished, Thomas pauses for a moment. He remembers time spent with his insignificant friend. He stammers to himself mawkishly,

"Goodbye my friend."

Then splits the sandwich. Thomas exits the kitchen to enter the bedroom with his snack.

Days go by. An intimate friendship waxes into love and brings us back to a local hospital. Thomas nervously waits in the hospital room with Laura and hears the sound of a baby's cry. The doctor gives the newborn to a nurse. The nurse gently cleanses the baby. The heart monitor changes its rhythm. One of the nurses recommends Thomas step outside for a moment as they make adjustments. Thomas rushes out of the room and throws both hands on the glass. He intently peers through the shades checking on Laura. He pays attention to the doctor and nurses inserting IV's into Laura's arms. At that very moment, his father walks up and stands behind Thomas questioning,

"How did everything go?"

Thomas grumbles,

"There seems to be a problem, Pa."

A nurse opens the door and gestures Thomas to enter the room. Thomas enters the room and the doctor sadly says to Thomas,

"Laura is hemorrhaging at a rate we can't control. Mr. Dalton, this is a sudden grief; I must inform you your beloved is fading. I suggest you say your goodbyes."

Thomas with a lump in his throat advances to Laura,

"I did not know we were going to do this so soon."

Laura mutters,

"Lauren."

Thomas leans in,

"What did you say?"

Laura speaks heavily,

"Lauren, I want you to name our daughter, Lauren."

Thomas asserts,

"You Got It...anything else?"

A tear rolls down Laura's cheek that meets her lips. She licks the tear and swallows before her last words,

"Say it."

Thomas somberly affirms,

"Goodbye My Love."

Thomas remains at bedside staring at the wooden headboard. After thirty minutes a nurse politely separates Thomas' hand from Laura's. Thomas goes outside.

His father stands near a pond and feeds the fish. Thomas sits on an iron bench. His father relaxes beside him knowing what transpired.

Thomas opens up,

"How does someone go on after being put through this?"

His father removes his cap,

"No one should have to. Moving on and going forward is a choice you can make. You may stay here and sulk in sorrow and have sadness prey on your mind, but those actions do not make you a better person; only the sentiment of wanting to do so does. Son, what I do know is you have a beauteous daughter to share your life with."

Thomas nods,

"But father there is a pit in my stomach which shall never diminish."

His father responds,

"Then turn the pit into a stone. A stone to help make life's pain impenetrable and carve into that stone the name of your Love."

Thomas gloomily heads back into the hospital lobby. A small girl runs past Thomas and dunks a young boy's head in a fountain. The two impishly scamper off as a nurse escorts Thomas down the hallway and points through a glass window,

"The third one from the left is your daughter.

Do you have a name for this child?"

Thomas feels anger but curbs this by making eye contact with the kind nurse, he draws a deep breath to answer,

"Lauren, her name will always be Lauren."

Thomas flattens his right hand on the glass. Baby Lauren lies in the crib. She presses her tiny hand against the acrylic crib; one Thomas surely knows he will never let go of.